This **Picture Mammoth** *belongs to*

_____

_____

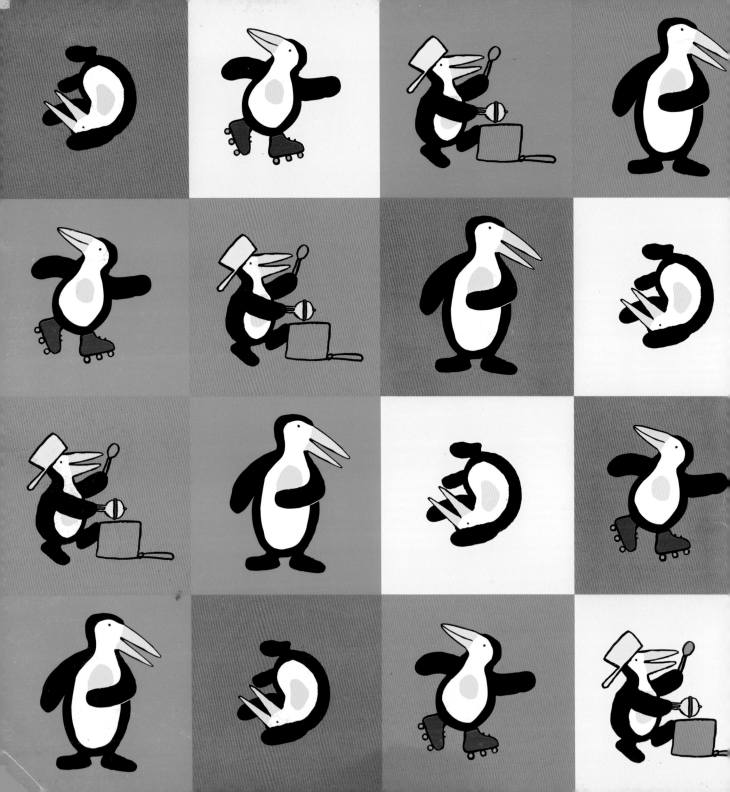

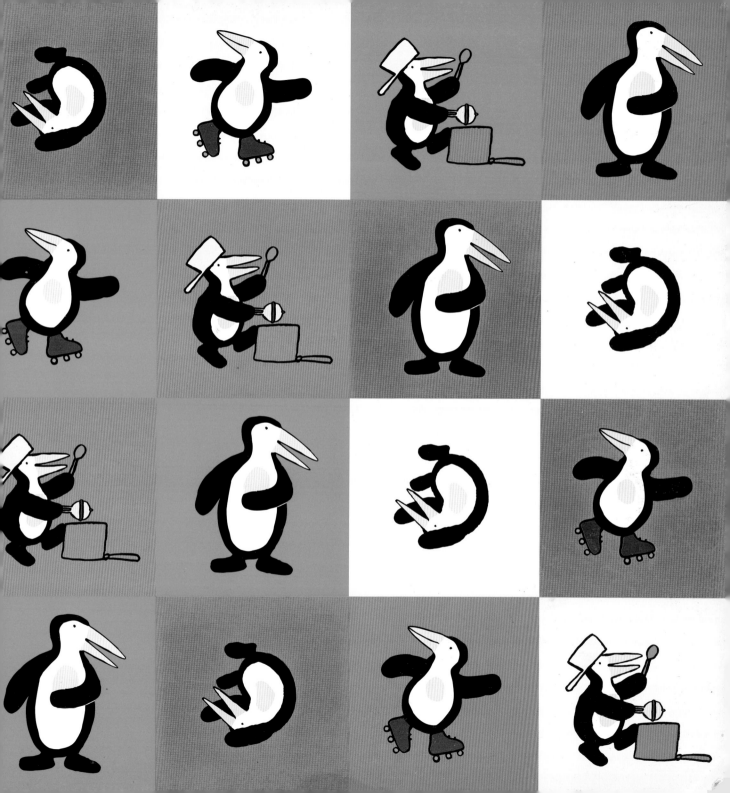

To my grandmother,
May Morris

First published in Great Britain 1998
by Methuen Children's Books Ltd
Published 1999 by Mammoth
an imprint of Egmont Children's Books Limited
239 Kensington High Street, London, W8 6SA
10 9 8 7 6 5 4 3

Copyright © Mary Murphy 1998
Mary Murphy has asserted her moral rights

ISBN 0 7497 3241 5

A CIP catalogue record for this title
is available from the British Library

Printed in Great Britain

Please be Quiet!

Mary Murphy

Picture mammoth

I drum on the pot

Bam!
Bam!
Rattle!

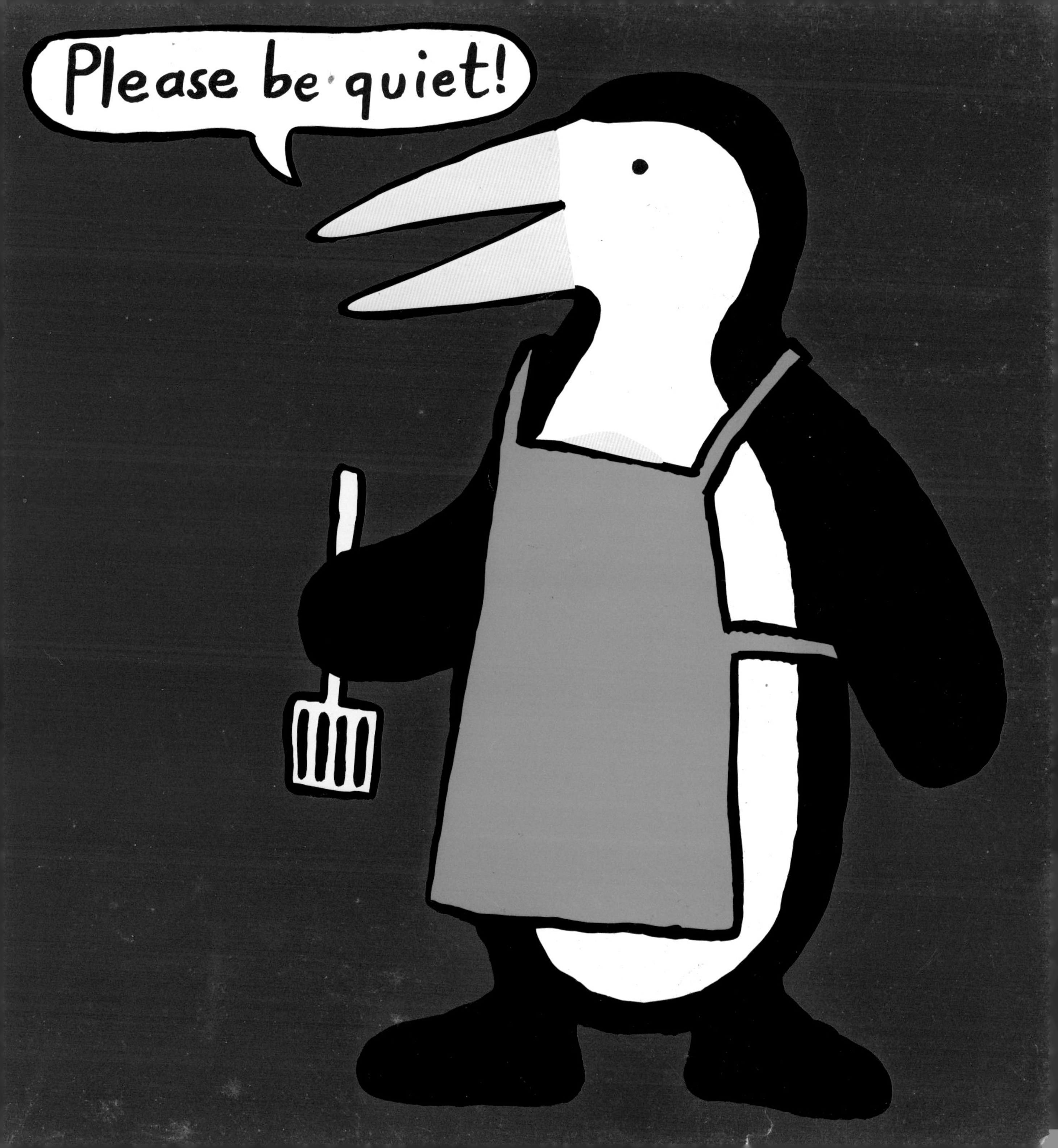
Please be quiet!

I bounce on the bed

Zoom!

Zoom!

I go really fast

I run down the path

thrup   thrup   thrup

I swing on the gate

I hop with my friends

thud

clatter

clunk

thump

We roll in the grass

I jump in a puddle.

splish

splosh

splash

I skip with socks on

hush

hush

hush

hush

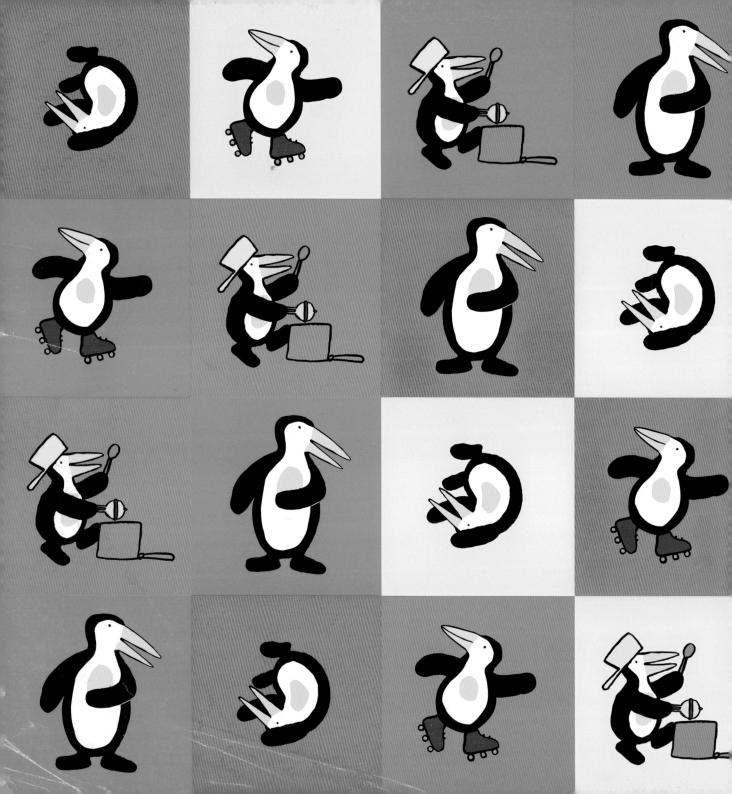

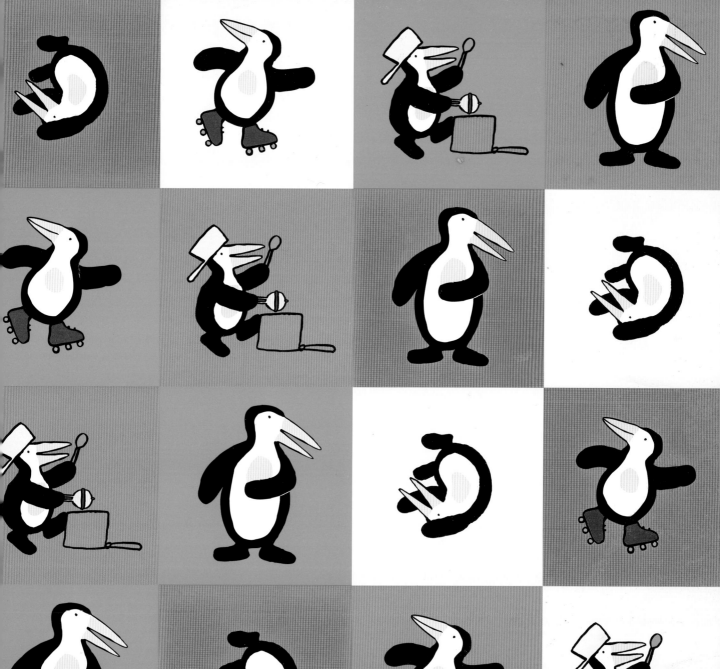